Dear Parents:

Congratulations! Your child is taking the first steps on an exciting journey. The destination? Independent reading!

STEP INTO READING® will help your child get there. The program offers five steps to reading success. Each step includes fun stories and colorful art or photographs. In addition to original fiction and books with favorite characters, there are Step into Reading Non-Fiction Readers, Phonics Readers and Boxed Sets, Sticker Readers, and Comic Readers—a complete literacy program with something to interest every child.

Learning to Read, Step by Step!

Ready to Read   Preschool–Kindergarten
• big type and easy words • rhyme and rhythm • picture clues
For children who know the alphabet and are eager to begin reading.

Reading with Help   Preschool–Grade 1
• basic vocabulary • short sentences • simple stories
For children who recognize familiar words and sound out new words with help.

Reading on Your Own   Grades 1–3
• engaging characters • easy-to-follow plots • popular topics
For children who are ready to read on their own.

Reading Paragraphs   Grades 2–3
• challenging vocabulary • short paragraphs • exciting stories
For newly independent readers who read simple sentences with confidence.

Ready for Chapters   Grades 2–4
• chapters • longer paragraphs • full-color art
For children who want to take the plunge into chapter books but still like colorful pictures.

STEP INTO READING® is designed to give every child a successful reading experience. The grade levels are only guides; children will progress through the steps at their own speed, deve_____g.

Remember, a lifetime love of reading start

D1041625

Visit us on the Web!
StepIntoReading.com
randomhousekids.com

Educators and librarians, for a variety of teaching tools, visit us at
RHTeachersLibrarians.com

ISBN 978-1-5247-1686-8 (trade) — ISBN 978-1-5247-1687-5 (lib. bdg.)

Printed in the United States of America

10 9 8 7 6 5 4 3 2 1

nickelodeon

RUSTY RIVETS

MEET RUSTY RIVETS!

by Mary Tillworth

illustrated by Donald Cassity

Random House 🏠 New York

Meet Rusty Rivets!
He loves to make things.
He loves to build
and invent.

Rusty invents
in his Rivet Lab.
His friends help.
Come and meet them!

Ruby is
Rusty's best friend.
Ruby has a tablet.
She uses it to help
Rusty invent.

Bytes is a robot dog.
Rusty and Ruby
built Bytes.
Bytes plays fetch!

The Bits
are Rusty's robot helpers.
Ruby can call them
with her tablet.

Ray is a flashlight.

His beam is bright.

He lights Rusty's way!

Crush is a clamp.

He holds tight

with his powerful jaw!

Whirly is a flying robot.
She can lift things
high into the air!

Jack is a forklift.

He is strong.

He gives Rusty a boost!

Rusty, Ruby, and the Bits
work together.
The friends hammer.
They drill.
They paint.

The friends build
a new robot.
His name is Botasaur.

Botasaur acts like a dog.

He plays fetch

with Bytes!

Liam is Rusty's neighbor.

He often gets into trouble.

Uh-oh!

Liam flies away.

Rusty and Ruby
invent a balloon popper.
Pop! Pop! Pop!
Rusty and Ruby save Liam!

Mr. Higgins
is an inventor, too!
He helps Rusty
find spare parts.

Chef Betty
owns a bakery.
She makes
cakes and cookies.

Ranger Anna loves animals.

She works at the animal park.

Rusty and Ruby visit her.

They visit the penguins, too!

Sammy Scoops runs
an ice cream shop.
Rusty and Ruby
stop by for a sweet treat!

Rusty has a party
in his yard!
His friends bring things
that they made—
cake, ice cream, and
a remote-control plane!

They celebrate together.

Hooray for friends!
Hooray for Rusty Rivets!